The Chew Crew

AF652837

Verses Kindler Publication

Verses Kindler Publication.
Website: www.verseskindlerpublication.com

The Chew Crew
By: Ms. Ruhi Swamy
ISBN: 978-93-49532-59-5
1st Edition
Price: INR 199/$13

Disclaimer

The Chew Crew is authored by Ruhi Swamy. The entirety of this published work comprises the original content of the author, who has undertaken diligent efforts in its editing. The characters depicted herein may be fictitious or inspired by real events; however, they are not intended to cause offense or represent any prejudice against any caste or system. Any similarity to the names of actual individuals, locations, or institutions is purely coincidental and serves the narrative. The author bears sole responsibility for the originality of this work; the publisher assumes no liability thereof.

Contents

Introduction

The Chew Crew live in a really big house with lots of space to run and play, inside and outside. They can go anywhere they want, except Jimmy, who stays in his tiny cage next to the big building. But don't worry—he still gets to watch everything that happens! They lived with, Ruhi and her parents. Ruhi is super kind and always gives them yummy treats, fun toys, and all sorts of surprises. Life with the Chew Crew is never boring—it's always an adventure! Come, lets meet the Crew!

July: Oldest of the chew crew. She is a calm dog and observes what's happening before attacking, unless it's her rusk being sniffed. She is the team's plan maker.

Boba: He is the second oldest in the crew. He is always excited to show everyone his toys. He loves to get belly rubs like all dogs and never waits to jump into a situation or game. He is the do-er of the team.

The triplets: They are an amazing group of triplet rats. They do all sorts of gymnastic moves, and are very fit and trained. They got rescued at a young age. They are:

Nora: The oldest of her sisters, Nora is a black rat who loves peace and quiet. Unlike her sisters, she knows how to read. She enjoys gymnastics, but she would skip it any day for a chance to visit the rat library her owner, Ruhi, promised to build. Because she can move so quietly, she steals all the treats from the cabinet—she's basically the team's ninja

Rainbow: The middle sister. She is a grey rat who attempts things no rat would try, whether it's a triple back flip or building the first rat rocket. She performs tricks her sisters cannot even think of. She is the one who helps in situations which need extreme precision. She is the nimble cat of the team. Ironic, isn't it?

Alice: She is the youngest of her sisters. She is a white rat who loves acting silly and funny. She is very good at dancing, squeak singing and tower building. Although she seems useless for the team, she is important for distracting the humans while the team performs operations. She is the distractor of the team.

Jimmy: He is not exactly part of the team, but he is still a pet. He is a rescued stray. He lives in a tiny cage and gets no toys or special treats. He always complains and tries to ruin the chew crew. He can easily manipulate the chew crew with his calm voice. He is street smart and can get what he wants from the other pets.

And a surprise member joining later in the story!

1

How Jimmy got caged

It was a rainy day, and the Chew Crew were inside the house. July sat on the black sofa, chewing a rusk. Boba was watching a cartoon on the TV. Rainbow was trying to make a pen that rats could use, and Nora watched the rain through the window.

Alice, on the other hand, was bored. She had already finished playing in the playhouse, practicing her gymnastics, dancing, and spending time with the others. Suddenly, she got an idea.

She gathered her group using the whistle Rainbow had made out of a plastic straw. "I am so bored!" she said. "I have a great idea, but I need your help. Will you help me?"

Boba answered first. "Last time you had an amazing idea, you got stuck in a cereal box."

"This time it's a good idea!" Alice said quickly. "I thought we could make a small story about an old memory of ours and turn it into a book—like a memoir or something."

"That's actually not a bad idea," July said.

"But how are we going to write it?" Boba asked. "Rainbow already made a mini book with scraps of paper and a paintbrush with cut-off Barbie hair, but we can't write in it because we don't have a pen!"

Rainbow replied in a silly voice, "What do you think I'm here for? I've been working on it while you were wasting time."

"Perfect! But we have many old memories. Which one should we write about?" Nora asked calmly.

Alice brightened. "Remember when Jimmy used to free roam and he was part of the Chew Crew? What if we write about how Jimmy got caged?"

Everyone agreed.

Nora got ready with a small desk made out of a thimble, a mini pen and book. Although Boba and July could write too, Nora had the best handwriting. Almost similar to Ruhi. Alice wanted to do the paintings, because she loved art. Everyone agreed because no one else wanted to paint. Nora began writing in her neatest handwriting:

"Many years ago, there were 6 free roam pets in Ruhi's house: July, Boba, Nora, Rainbow, Alice and Jimmy. Before he got caged, Jimmy was part of the newly formed Chew Crew too. He went on all their missions, just like a normal member. He knew the crew did not have a leader, and he was fine with that, until one day. It was a normal Chew Crew mission in which they were trying to catch a chipmunk that was stealing July's rusk. Just when the chipmunk was about to run away with July's whole packet of rusk, Jimmy caught her. He quickly jumped as high as he could, and grabbed the chipmunk's tail in his mouth.

He gently placed her on the ground along with the rusk and talked her into giving it back but he was kind enough to also give the chipmunk a small bite so that she doesn't go hungry. "She will ask for it next time rather than steal", said Jimmy. July was very happy and so were the others. "You have actually done well this time, Jimmy!" Rainbow said.

Nora's mouth was hung open, and Alice said, "Wow Jimmy, that was actually smart!"

Boba gave him a happy tail wag and said, "Good job! You really completed the mission for us!".

July didn't say anything, but she was jumping around, her tail wagging so fast it made a "whoosh" sound in the air.

Jimmy was proud to be a big help to the team. Soon, he became overconfident and decided that he should be the team's leader. One rainy day, he called everyone to the big playhouse using the whistle Rainbow had made out of a used straw. Everyone rushed to the playhouse Ruhi had built.

"What happened, Jimmy? Is everything okay?" July asked, ready to plan their next mission.

"I have a suggestion," Jimmy said. "I think the Chew Crew needs a leader—someone to guide them, plan their missions, and choose what they do. We have a great team, but it would be even better with a great leader."

Everyone looked confused, but no one said a word.

"I think," Jimmy continued, "that the leader should be me, because I was so helpful during the last mission and made sure, we didn't go rusk-free. I would lead the team the way a great team should be lead."

Alice immediately burst into her silly laugh. July signaled for her to be quiet and spoke in a calm but scary voice. "Jimmy, what are you thinking? You helped us in one mission and suddenly think you're our king? You know the Chew Crew will never have a leader. We all have our own roles."

Playful Boba had a serious expression on his face. "Jimmy, July is right. You cannot be our leader, but you will always be very important to our team. Here, everyone is equally important."

The others agreed. Jimmy was not upset. Instead, he decided that if he showed them what a great leader he could be, the others would eventually listen.

Their next mission was to get Boba's toy which had got stuck on a tree because of a bird who thought it was food. While July was explaining the plan, Jimmy pushed her aside and said, "Let me handle this mission, July." He began explaining a very confusing plan, and the other members had to do all the work while he just had to sit and watch. The others didn't try to argue, because they knew that Jimmy was the master at getting what he wants. They just went along with Jimmy's plan, with Alice complaining quietly the whole time. The next few missions went similarly, with Jimmy bossing them around and had also started punishing them for any misses. The Chew Crew soon got tired of it. They held a secret meeting without Jimmy and agreed that they should tell him that if he doesn't stop bossing them around, they would kick him out of the Crew.

One evening, Alice blew her whistle. The whole Crew arrived. Everyone knew this was part of the plan—except Jimmy. They walked into the house and gathered in the living room. Then they sat in a circle on the floor.

"Jimmy, we have something to tell you," Alice said.
"Something important," Nora added.

"Yes, I know," Jimmy said. "And I agree. No one should have a whistle except me, because I am the Crew's great leader!"

"About that… it's about that," Rainbow said softly.

"Jimmy," Boba said, "we've noticed that you've been acting a little bossy lately. I understand that you're happy and confident about planning, and you want to feel important. But you're being *too* bossy."

July spoke again in her calm-but-scary voice. "Boba was being kind. You're not a little bossy—you're very bossy. And if you don't stop, we will kick you out of the Chew Crew."

Jimmy was angry. But he had a plan—a plan so evil that only he could come up with it. First, he needed to apologize.

"I am so sorry!" he said. "I didn't realize it. I'll try to change from now on."

The Crew was happy. They ended the meeting and went to get snacks.

The next day was when Jimmy planned to put his idea into action. He thought it was perfect. His plan was to spread fake news about everyone in the group.

He walked up to playful Boba, who was chasing a butterfly.
"Hey, Boba, good morning!"
"Good morning, Jimmy!"

Jimmy said, "I saw something… something bad. July and Rainbow were talking about you. They agreed that you slow the team down, and they're planning to hold a meeting to kick you out. You might want to be careful around those two."

"I'm never talking to them again! Thank you for telling me," Boba said. He stopped chasing the butterfly and went inside the house to watch his cartoon.

"Perfect," Jimmy thought to himself.

He spread even more false news throughout the day, making everyone angry at each other—everyone except Jimmy. A few days later, the whole Crew became moody. The triplets didn't pay attention when Ruhi tried to teach them a trick, July didn't eat her rusk, and Boba stopped wagging his tail happily when Ruhi came back from school.

Ruhi knew something was wrong, but she didn't know what.

A week later, the Crew was so frustrated that they started attacking humans just to let out their anger. Ruhi knew she had been right from the start—something was definitely going on. She needed to figure out what.

She put all the members in cages for a little while because of the attacks—everyone except Jimmy. She talked to her parents and checked the security cameras around the house. She also found some sticky notes in Jimmy's bed and tried to match them with what she saw on the cameras.

After a day of investigating, she understood Jimmy's plan. She sat down to talk to him. He admitted everything, but only because Ruhi had so much proof.

"Jimmy, this is too much!" she said. "I'm going to have to keep you in a cage permanently."

Jimmy got ready to attack, but luckily the others stopped him just in time.

By the end of the day, Jimmy was placed in a cage—where he still stays today—complaining and howling. The Chew Crew is now only five members, but they are happy. Everyone still treats Jimmy kindly because they pity him, even though he was mean, and because he is family too."

Nora finished writing and gave the book to Alice so she could color and paint the pictures. When they were done, they gave it to Ruhi, who loved it. She said she had forgotten how Jimmy was caged, and that their story reminded her.

2

Jimmy's worst idea

It was a hot, sunny day, yet the Chew Crew decided to play outside. Nora only agreed because the rest of the team let her sit under a tree and read The Pink Rat, her favorite book. Rainbow wanted to learn a new trick, and Alice decided to help her. Boba was being his silly self, hopping around a tree and pretending to be a squirrel.

July soon began regretting her decision to play outside. She was feeling peckish and wanted some rusk.
"I'm hungry," she said. "Let's get some food from the kitchen! Who's with me?"

Boba, always ready for food, said, "I'm ready! I wanted some kibble anyway."
The triplets agreed and sent Alice to distract the humans with a new dance she had learned so they could sneak some snacks out quietly.

From his cage, Jimmy shouted, 'Take me with you! I want a treat for once.' As usual, everyone ignored him and went inside. When they came back after a successful mission, they had their paws full of food.

Jimmy was jealous, as always. He came up with a plan to get himself a snack, but he didn't think anyone would help him. Using the long nail he had been growing; he slipped his paw under the latch and opened it. He was free!

Alice, who was helping Rainbow decorate her car, saw this and yelled, "Code brown! The prisoner Jimmy is free!"

Nora just laughed and teased Alice. "Wow! Some baby was paying attention in code class!"

July shook her head. "No, she's telling the truth!"

Jimmy ran out the main gate and onto the road. The road was busy, and no one ever dared put their paws there without Ruhi.

"We have to save him!" Boba cried.

The group had mixed feelings—Alice and Rainbow agreed with him, while Nora and July disagreed. In the end, they decided they had to go anyway.

Alice sat in an old shoebox tied to Boba's back paw, while Rainbow sat on his back and Nora rode on July's. Together, they rushed out of the gate as fast as their paws could carry them.

Jimmy was having an argument with a stray dog on the road. He lost the argument and was about to get attacked, so he ran away, carelessly dashing across the busy street. A speeding car screeched and braked just in time to avoid hitting him. The loud screech terrified him and brought him back to his senses. Seeing how busy and unsafe the road was, he realized all he wanted was to go home and lock himself in his cage—but now he was lost.

As he wandered aimlessly, he accidentally bumped into a tall man wearing a t-shirt that said, *"The Stray Stays Away!"*

Unaware of the man's intentions, Jimmy squealed with hope. The man grabbed him and placed him into a small cage next to many other stray dogs in a dark, dingy room behind his store, where he sold butcher knives.

Meanwhile, the Chew Crew searched every familiar corner in vain. July struggled to think of a plan. Suddenly, an idea struck her.

"Boba, try to sniff Jimmy out. You're a Labrador, so your nose is stronger than mine."

Boba began sniffing, with the rest of the crew following him. When he finally stopped, he said, "One of these dogs is him. There are too many, and I can't tell which one from far away."

Nora hopped off July's back. "I think I know which one he is!" she squeaked. "I've read many books, and I know that stray dogs never have collars. This one is him!" She pointed confidently.

"There's still a problem," July said. "This man won't let us free him. But I have a plan. Alice, you know what to do—distract him. Rainbow, the keys are on top of the cage. It's very tall, so I need you to do a special gymnastic move to grab them and unlock the cage. I'll make sure no crowd gathers here. Boba, help me. Nora, ride on Boba's back!"

Boba and July moved into position. Alice began a cute dance to distract the man. Everyone was nervous—it was their first rescue mission—but Rainbow was the most scared. She loved doing the impossible, but no one had ever relied on her to succeed in such a dangerous move, especially with the cage so tall.

Taking a deep breath, Rainbow jumped. She performed a triple backflip, soaring higher and higher. Midair, she rolled to land on the cage. From above, it looked like she would fall and break her neck, and she felt as terrified as a mouse trapped in a cat cage. But she landed perfectly on her hind legs. For a brief moment, she felt proud—but there was no time to celebrate. She quickly jumped down and unlocked the cage.

Jimmy barked with joy as he was freed. Rainbow signaled for him to stay quiet and sat on his back to guide him. July and Boba ran back with Nora on Boba's back, while Alice rode in the shoebox. Everyone was happy the mission had succeeded, but no one said a word—they were all too tired.

On the way home, they looked at the sky, now glowing orange as the streetlights flicked on. On one lamp post, Ruhi noticed a poster of a missing dog. The picture looked exactly like Jimmy. It said a dog had been rescued, and now his parents were looking for him.

Jimmy's eyes widened. "Oh! My parents remember me!"

"That's you?" Ruhi asked. "Your parents are looking for you?"

Jimmy vaguely remembered being stolen from his family and running away from the gruff, smelly man who laughed after kicking him. Ruhi's eyes filled with tears as they all walked home, realizing someone else had loved Jimmy just as much before she did.

When they reached home, Jimmy locked himself inside his cage, with the Chew Crew surrounding him. He looked confused. "Why did you save me even though I'm so mean to you?"

The Crew didn't answer—and Jimmy didn't ask again. He knew they were too tired to explain.

The next day, the Crew sat on the lawn, keeping their voices low.

"Remember the poster we saw yesterday?" Nora said. "I think we should just let Jimmy go. He's pretty mean to us."

"But you saw Ruhi crying yesterday!" Boba said. "Even though he's mean, he's still her pet."

"I think we should let her decide later," July said. "Let's not worry about it now."

They all went inside to play, unaware that Jimmy had been listening the entire time.

3

The Chew Crew vs The Robot Pets

It was an ordinary, quiet day. The Chew Crew hadn't had any missions for a whole week—no treat-grabbing missions, no squirrel-catching missions, and not even "stop Jimmy" missions. In short, they were bored. Even Nora, who usually loved lazy days, was bored.

Rainbow had an idea—not one of her usual impossible or strange inventions, just a normal, boring idea.

"I'm so bored," she said. "What if we go to the playhouse and see if there's anything unusual waiting for us? Maybe we'll find something to do."

Everyone agreed. It was probably better than lying in the grass, wondering what to do next. When they arrived, there *was* something unusual waiting for them.

To reach the big playhouse on the second floor, they had to walk across the living room. There, they saw a package covered in neon pink paper.

"What does it say? Tell me! I don't know how to read!" Alice squeaked, her silly voice returning.

July read aloud, "It says, *'Free Gift,'* and it's from The Robotic Pets Lab (RPL)—the future of pets!"

"That's weird… a free gift! I wonder what's inside," Nora said.

"It's our job to give the parcels to Ruhi," Boba said as he walked toward her room, placing the package on the floor by the bed. "Let's do it without worrying too much."

"Maybe we can go to the playhouse and play cards!" Rainbow suggested as they finished delivering the parcels.

After many rounds of cards, the Crew came back to the living room and saw Ruhi and her parents assembling something with a lot of metal parts. The pink box was beside them.

Nora, who had read books about robots, said, "I think they're building a robot pet. The parts and wires look just like the ones in a robot, and the box is from a pet lab."

Rainbow and Alice were thinking the same thing, but only Rainbow asked aloud, "Why would they need a robot pet when they already have us?"

July added, "It looks like they've finished two dog-like robots and are building a rat robot. Maybe they're meant as gifts for us?"

Boba tilted his head. "Then why would it say it's a free gift? A gift for whom? I may not read as many books as Nora, but I know from stories that you never really know what's inside a free gift!"

They were all very confused. No one said anything—except Alice, who wanted to taste the robots. "If it tastes good, it's our friend!" she said. Everyone rolled their eyes and went outside.

At dinnertime, the Chew Crew came back inside to see five robots walking around the house—three rats and two dogs.

Almost as if she read their minds, Ruhi walked up to them. "Don't be scared! They're just our new robots—Julia, Bobby, Alli, Rina, and Nona. They're my pets, and you five better be nice to them! Or else you'll end up in cages like Jimmy!"

Everyone was shocked. Ruhi was always kind, but it felt like the robots were replacing them. After dinner, the five of them went to Ruhi's bedroom and saw her holding a talent show with the robots. She was having a blast! Rainbow was the most upset—Ruhi hadn't invited them to join.

The next day, everyone watched Alli dance. Alice tried to reclaim her spot by dancing even better, but everyone called her distracting. The robots continued taking over the Crew's usual jobs—bringing parcels, dancing, even removing people's socks—and the Chew Crew felt replaced every time Ruhi clapped for the robots.

The following day, Ruhi went to a restaurant for dinner with her parents. The restaurant had a pet-friendly menu, so the Chew Crew went along, while Ruhi brought the robots.

Just as they were about to order, a waiter ran out screaming, "Everyone get out! The kitchen is on fire!" Ruhi and her family grabbed the robots and ran, forgetting the Crew, who followed anyway.

After the building was empty, July's ears perked up. She heard faint barking. "Hey! Someone left their dog in there! We have to save him. Here's the plan: cover ourselves in sand so we don't get burned. Jump through the window. There's a fire extinguisher—triplets, jump over the fire and grab it. Balance it on your backs. Boba, help us. If the dog is surrounded by fire, extinguish it. I'll get the dog, and we'll jump out as fast as possible."

The Crew rolled in sand at a construction site beside the restaurant. A woman was crying because she'd left her poodle in a purse. Ruhi saw the Crew preparing to jump and shouted, "No! Come back here, please!"

Inside the restaurant, covered in sand, the Crew saw the poodle in the purse on a table surrounded by fire. Nora, Rainbow, and Alice jumped high to reach the extinguisher, standing on top of each other. They grabbed it, threw it down, and quickly extinguished the fire.

Boba spotted the purse and the small, scared white head of the dog inside. He helped July carry the extinguisher while she picked up the purse with the poodle. Together, they ran out through the window.

The woman was overjoyed to get her dog back, and so was Ruhi. She hugged them tightly, even though they were covered in sand. "I am never going to let you do that again!" she said.

Ruhi was proud of the Crew, especially since the robots had gotten their wires melted in the smoke. The Chew Crew was proud of their second rescue mission and happy the robots were gone. When they got home, they were treated to an extra-special dinner, and Ruhi built a small pet park outside so they wouldn't get bored. Everyone was thrilled with how things had turned out.

4

Happy Birthday July

It was the 22nd of June. July's birthday was the next day. The Chew Crew didn't know it was her birthday because she had never told them. But they overheard Ruhi talking to her parents about it. Ruhi had asked if she could throw a small party for July, but her parents said no.

Alice's eyes widened. "Everyone deserves a birthday party!" she said sadly.

Everyone agreed with her. July, who had overheard them too, shrugged. "Birthdays aren't important. What matters is having more Chew Crew missions. So, no plans for my birthday."

The Crew knew exactly what to do. Nora took over as planner this time. She instructed everyone to grab a rusk from the kitchen to distract July while they secretly planned her party.

July sat chewing her rusk on the black sofa, unaware, while the rest of the Crew rolled in the soft grass on the lawn and discussed the party.

"I know July is the oldest member of the Crew, but that's no reason not to celebrate her birthday too!" Nora said.

Boba wagged his tail in agreement.

"Let's give her the best birthday party ever!" Alice exclaimed. "Let's do it in the new park Ruhi built for us—it's perfect!"

Rainbow raised a paw. "I love the plan, but who will host it? Someone has to plan decorations, invitations, food, and games."

They considered everyone carefully:

> Alice? Too silly—she'd make the whole party about dancing unicorns.
>
> Rainbow? Her plan would be amazing, but it would be impossible to actually do it.
>
> Boba? He'd focus only on food, and no one would eat for a week!
>
> Nora? She knew a lot from her books and could make quiet, doable plans. But was she fun? Nobody knew, yet they elected her anyway.

Nora, usually the quiet one, jumped onto a rock like a podium to give instructions.

"Here's the plan," she said. "We have to do this without July knowing. Today, we invite friends, get snacks, and plan the games. Tomorrow, we decorate. We can ask Ruhi for help—if we ask nicely, she might assist since she was planning to have a party too.

Alice, you're on distraction duty. Keep July busy so we can plan. If she comes back, distract her. Bring her here at exactly 4:30 pm.

Rainbow, you're the decoration team. Plan the design today. Tomorrow, use your gymnastic skills to help decorate with my help—or with Ruhi's if she comes.

Boba, you're on food. Use your cuteness and voice to get Ruhi to help with rusk and dog treats.

Go, everyone! Alice, stay with me and help plan the games."

Everyone went to work. Alice and Nora planned and arranged games. Boba convinced Ruhi to help with food. Rainbow worked on decorations using waste paper and popped balloons, sealed with tape.

Just minutes later, July walked out of the house.

"Nora!" whispered Alice. She ran to July and led her back inside, pretending she wanted to show her a new dance. The rest of the Crew continued their secret preparations.

With July distracted, Boba persuaded Ruhi to help with food and borrow leftover decorations from her previous birthday. Nora made a list of games: tag, hide and seek, Ring the Rusk, Lucky Draw (where only July would win), and Hopscotch.

Alice asked Ruhi, "Why aren't your parents letting you celebrate July's birthday?"

Ruhi replied, "They said it's a waste of time celebrating a pet's birthday. If I want to, I have to do it on my own."

Nora walked over. "There's no time to stand around. Let me see what you've done."

Rainbow had planned pink and blue balloons and a big purple banner with "July" on it. Alice had lulled July to sleep with a soft lullaby. Everything was ready—they just had to keep it a secret until tomorrow.

The next day arrived. It was July's birthday. Everyone pretended to forget, but they were all excited. Alice immediately took July to the playhouse after breakfast, keeping her busy until 4:30 pm. Meanwhile, Ruhi and Rainbow decorated the park, using both Rainbow's handmade decorations and Ruhi's supplies. Boba went to the kitchen to fetch rusk, dog treats, and cucumbers. Nora handed out invitations to July's friends—Dollie the Dalmatian, Ruby the Rottweiler, Crazie the alley cat, and Nutso the squirrel.

July grew bored of Alice and wanted to go outside. Alice couldn't let her, since it was only 4:00 pm. She came up with a clever plan: a blindfolded walk to the park. "If I promise to let you go after this, will you play one last game?" Alice said. July reluctantly agreed.

At 4:20, guests began arriving. The park was ready. Nora climbed a big rock, holding a straw like a microphone.

"Okay, everyone! The party is ready, but we're missing one thing—July, the birthday girl! She will arrive at 4:30 with Alice."

As if on cue, Alice led blindfolded July to the rock. She removed the blindfold, and everyone shouted, "Happy Birthday, July!"

July was amazed. She had never had a birthday celebration before. She played games, especially ring the rusk, and ate treats. For the cake cutting, Ruhi brought a big tower of rusk. July carefully took pieces for everyone, sharing happily.

Dollie whispered, "July, why are you called July if you were born in June?"

July smiled. "I was a birthday gift for Ruhi, and her birthday is in July. She thought of funny names like Ninini, Moo, and Lalaa, but finally chose July because she got me in July."

Everyone nodded, a little confused, then went on to play more party games. At 6:00 pm, the party ended.

July hugged the Crew tightly. "Thank you! I had an amazing time!"

Nora smiled. "We're having a party next time too, right?"

"Yes!" Boba agreed.

“I’ll be the host next time!” Alice said excitedly.

Rainbow teased, “She’d be perfect if you want a party with dancing and pink unicorns!”

July laughed. “That would be perfect!” Everyone laughed and walked happily into the house.

5

The Pet Fest

It was a normal day for the Chew Crew in Ruhi's house. A week had passed since they celebrated July's birthday. With no missions or vacations that week, everyone was busy with their usual routines.

Boba was trying to get Ruhi's attention by showing her toys, but she was too busy with homework.

July was acting cute, hoping someone would give her a rusk, but she was ignored. When she tried to take one herself, everyone noticed.

Nora was writing a book about boats, but kept getting interrupted by Alice practicing her backflips. (She almost always landed on Nora's head as a joke.)

Rainbow was building a car for rats using old batteries for the engine, a jar for the body, cloth and sponge for the seat, buttons for the steering wheel, wheels, and rubber bands to hold it all together.

They continued with their activities until Ruhi stepped onto the lawn and called all the pets together.

"Tomorrow," she announced, "we're going somewhere special just for you! We're going to the Pet Fest! There will be games with prizes, treats, and shows. I've entered you all in the show because I know you'll win! But there's one thing: I'll only be with you during the show at 6:30 p.m. The rest of the time I'll be at the Honey Museum, because owners are only allowed with their pets during the show. Many people are hiring caretakers, so I have too. Tomorrow, after I drop you off, your caretaker Ms. Quincy, will look after you. I trust you five. Now, come in for dinner in a few minutes!"

The Chew Crew were delighted and quickly finished what they were doing before heading in for dinner.

The next day, Ruhi woke up early to get the Crew ready. She bathed Boba and July in an inflatable pool and washed the triplets in soup bowls. She scrubbed them neatly, dried them with towels, and used a hairdryer carefully so their fur wouldn't fluff up.

She combed Boba's and July's fur with a blue pet comb that had a button to remove extra hair, and brushed the triplets' fur with a soft toothbrush. She gave Boba and July socks made from balloons and tiny shoes from a shop so their paws wouldn't get dirty. Boba got a new dark blue collar with his name on it, and July a red one. She even made tail socks from old socks that didn't fit her.

For the triplets, she cut the fingertips off a rubber glove to make shoes. She gave them waist straps with hooks for leashes, each labeled with their names. Finally, they all sat in the car and left.

At the fair, Ruhi led them to their caretaker and said goodbye. The Chew Crew were excited by the sight of the big festival. Ms. Quincy, their caretaker, had long blonde hair, bright green eyes, a white top, blue jeans, and a lace jacket. She looked nice—but she wasn't!

"Ugh, there are five of you! And rats too? I hate rats," she complained. "I can't take care of all of you. Either I take care of one and let the others go free, or I give you to another caretaker. I guess I'll take the squeaky dog and let the rest of you go."

The Chew Crew didn't like Ms. Quincy, but they had to listen. July stayed with her, while the others said goodbye and ran into the fest.

Inside, they saw many games—and many caretakers being mean to pets. Some refused to feed dogs if they drooled, abandoned cats for stepping on their legs, refused to take rats or hamsters at all, and even pulled tails if pets misbehaved.

The Crew realized it wasn't just Ms. Quincy—all the caretakers were cruel! They stayed silent until Boba spoke.

"We have to do something! They're hurting the pets."

Nora replied, "But we need July's help to make plans! The Chew Crew can't work without her."

Playful Alice tried to be serious. "We can each go our own way and meet at 6:00pm to practice for the show. We have to win, no matter what!"

Rainbow nodded. "Alice is right. We should help quietly so caretakers don't notice."

"But who will do what?" Alice asked. "Without July, this will be harder."

Nora giggled. "That's why you have a rat who can read! While we entered, I hopped onto the reception desk and read the book. I knew Boba or July couldn't jump that high."

Rainbow shouted, "What did you read? Tell us already!"

"Excluding us," Nora explained, "there are 40 pets here: 15 dogs, 5 rats, 10 cats, 7 rabbits, and 3 hamsters."

Boba said, "I'll take 10 dogs."

Rainbow added, "I'll help 5 dogs and 5 rats."

Alice said, "I'll help 10 cats."

Nora concluded, "I'll help 7 rabbits and 3 hamsters."

They split up.

Nora saw a caretaker holding two hamsters by their ears. She leapt onto the caretaker, caught a ball the shopkeeper threw, and whispered to the hamsters, "Don't worry." Terrified, the caretaker dropped them. Nora flipped down, caught them, and set them free.

Rainbow saw a caretaker pulling a husky's tail. She jumped on him and tickled him with her tail until he laughed and let go. Alice saw a caretaker teasing a hungry cat with treats. She climbed his leg, grabbed the bag, tossed it to the cat, and ran away.

Boba saw a caretaker trying to ride a young German Shepherd. He licked her arm until bubbles formed.

Disgusted, she left to wash her hand, giving the dog time to escape.

Meanwhile, July was winning games and collecting prizes for the Crew.

By 6:00 pm, they reunited for practice. Alice helped July escape Ms. Quincy by jumping on her face, making her scream loudly. At 6:15 pm, Ruhi returned and helped them rehearse.

When it was time for the show, Ruhi wished them good luck and sat in the front row. Many pets were cute but didn't perform tricks- they just sat there.

The Chew Crew amazed the crowd - The triplets performed gymnastics, Boba walked on two legs while balancing a toy on his nose July squeaked a tune.

The audience loved them.

At 7:00 pm, the results were announced: The Chew Crew had won first place! They received a two-year supply of food and treats, many toys, and even dipped their paws in paint to sign a special paper.

Most of all, they were happy to have helped so many pets.

6

Roxy

It was the 3rd of July, the day before Ruhi's birthday. She was having an early birthday party with her friends and family. The Chew Crew had to stay in the pet playroom because some guests were scared of rats and dogs. They were told to stay quiet so they wouldn't distract anyone.

"Not fair!" Alice mumbled, before Nora quickly shushed her. Rainbow was sad because she couldn't practice gymnastics or build anything—it was "too noisy." Boba, trying to be goofy, gave a speech about plastic toys to a sleepy July and a pile of stuffed animals.

Finally, when the party ended at 7pm, the Crew could come out for dinner.

At the dining table, they saw colorful, shiny gifts stacked beside a potted plant. Everyone's eyes were on July as she tried to jump onto the tower of gifts.

"No, July! Eat your dinner instead of my gifts!" Ruhi scolded.

When July joined the other pets, they noticed a big bag of new toys, clothes, and treats on the table.

"Yay! Is that for us?" Boba and Alice shouted together.

Ruhi smiled. "No, but there's something that might surprise you!" She knelt beside them and pointed to a green basket in the corner. At first, everyone thought it was another gift—until it moved.

They thought they were imagining things, but then they knew it was real when they heard the basket sneeze. Ruhi walked up to the basket and opened it. A frightened whimper came from inside. A little black face peeked out from the fur. Ruhi lifted the puppy gently.

"Chew Crew," she said, "this is your new sister, Roxy. She's a Labrador, like you, Boba. She's still a puppy, so her bones are weak. She can join the Crew, but only for small missions for now. I know you'll all be good with her. Now, let's eat."

Ruhi pulled out three bowls for Boba, July, and Jimmy, filling them with rice and beans.

"Ugh, rice and beans again?" Boba grumbled.

"I hate rice and beans! I know it's healthy, but it tastes worse than Jimmy's socks!" July exclaimed.

Then Ruhi brought out three small bowls for the triplets, filled with watermelon and banana salad.

"But Ruhi, you promised us rusk and cucumber today!" Alice said sadly.

Nora added, "It was supposed to be the good food today!"

Rainbow asked, "Where's our rusk?"

Ruhi explained, "I know I promised, but there wasn't much rusk. I fed most of it to the pigeons in the park, since bird feed was finished, and gave the rest to Roxy when she arrived. Please adjust with this."

The Crew grumbled. Nora noticed, "Wait. Including Roxy, there are seven of us. But Ruhi only kept food for six. Where's the last bowl?"

Right on cue, Ruhi pulled out a brand-new bowl decorated with hearts and the name "Roxy."

They all thought the same thing: *How come she gets a new bowl?*

Ruhi mashed rice into a soft paste and topped it with pieces of chicken and powdered rusk. She even brought out some cucumbers and put it in the corner of the bowl.

July gasped. "This is the dinner we all wanted! How come she gets it and we don't?"

Boba's mouth dropped open.

Dinner was very quiet that night. When bedtime came, the Crew walked to their beds in the living room—but Roxy didn't follow. She went straight to Ruhi's room. The Crew couldn't believe it. None of them slept that night.

The next morning, after breakfast, the Crew gathered under the big Shuli tree in the backyard. A gentle breeze made Shuli flowers fall around them.

"Alright everyone. This is an official Chew Crew meeting," Alice declared, trying to sound important. Rainbow was so serious she didn't even do her usual handstands.

"Roxy is evil! She's trying to replace us!" Rainbow stomped her foot.

"Calm down," Nora said. "Maybe Roxy is good."

July agreed. "Nora is right. But Rainbow has a point too. We need to talk to her."

Boba added, "We should stay calm. If we're extra good, maybe we won't get replaced."

Just then, Roxy walked by, her black fur shining in the sun. She was about the size of a cabbage.

July whispered quickly, "She's coming! Alice, Boba, Nora—go act extra good inside the house. Rainbow and I will deal with Roxy."

The three ran inside. Roxy tried to run like Boba but tripped and landed on her nose. Rainbow giggled. July shook her head. "Can't even run properly," she muttered.

Rainbow forced a smile. "Hi Roxy! We were just going to meet Jimmy!"

July clenched her teeth. "Yes, the dog who never showers, chews shoes, and—"

Rainbow interrupted, "We're going to meet him, so bye!"

Roxy raised a paw. "But wait, I wanted to ask you something!"

Inside the house, Nora, Alice, and Boba cleaned the playroom, threw away rusk crumbs on the balcony, and removed Jimmy's sweater hidden behind a plant. No one noticed their efforts.

Later that evening, Alice danced in front of Ruhi. Roxy jumped onto the table and tried to copy her. Ruhi stopped watching Alice and focused on Roxy.

Boba quickly grabbed his toy to distract Ruhi, thinking it worked—until Roxy returned holding July's stuffed doll. Ruhi laughed and pet Roxy.

Rainbow and Nora flipped behind the table, but Roxy tried to copy them too. July wagged her tail in circles like a helicopter, and Roxy copied that as well, earning even more attention.

Before dinner, the Crew pulled Roxy behind a cupboard.

"Why do you want to replace us?" Nora asked.

"Replace you? What?" Roxy looked confused.

"Stop it. You know what we mean," Boba said.

"Just because you're small and cute doesn't mean you're better than us!" July added.

"I really don't know what you're saying," Roxy replied.

"You keep copying whatever we do!" Rainbow accused. "And somehow look cuter than us!" Alice added.

Roxy stepped back. "Are you feeling left out because of me?"

"Wasn't it obvious?" July rolled her eyes.

Roxy's ears drooped. "I'm so sorry! I just want to be like you. Where I was born, my siblings and I saw you as celebrities for being brave and saving people. When I first saw you, I was delighted to live with you! I think Ruhi gives me special treatment because I'm not as smart or trained as you. I need help just to run. I didn't mean to make you feel bad. Could you help me be like you—or even join the Chew Crew? Please?"

The Crew felt terrible. They had been nasty to her when she only wanted to belong.

After a long silence, Boba spoke. "I think you'd be perfect in the Crew, Roxy."

Nora added, "You can definitely join, but we'll find your role when you're older."

Alice said, "We'll include you in bigger missions later. We don't want you to get hurt."

Nora promised, "We'll be the best big siblings for you." July smiled. "Welcome to the Chew Crew, Roxy!"

From that day on, Roxy became more familiar and comfortable with the Crew. She started receiving normal treatment and began training in basic tricks. The Crew were happy—and they knew their future adventures would be even brighter.

7

Bye Bye Jimmy

It was a sunny day. The Crew were watching TV when Ruhi walked across the living room holding a leash.

Boba got excited. He jumped off the sofa and sat in front of her, thinking he was going for a walk. Ruhi laughed.

“Boba! This leash is not for you. I’m taking Jimmy to a dog playdate so he can meet other dogs.”

Boba looked disappointed as Ruhi continued toward Jimmy to put on the leash.

After a short walk, Ruhi and Jimmy arrived at a small building with a lush green lawn outside. Many dogs were already playing there. Ruhi dropped Jimmy off and began walking back home.

Jimmy quickly became popular for his calm face. He made friends with a pug named Pines, a poodle named Polly, and a golden retriever puppy named Goldie.

The dogs were cared for by a kind young woman named Jenny. She was about twenty, with long dark hair and brown eyes. Jenny welcomed each dog with a treat, petted them lovingly, and promised to feed and look after them for the day.

The morning passed quickly as Jimmy played with his new friends. He was having a wonderful time, though he had secret plans for the night that he hadn’t told anyone.

At lunch, the dogs were served a tasty meal - One bowl of milk with dried chicken pellets, another bowl of rice with chicken and for dessert, banana and apple salad

Jenny gave them water and then went for a walk. Goldie wanted more water, but Jenny wasn't there. She asked Jimmy for help, but he told her to wait until Jenny returned. Goldie was too thirsty to wait. She went to the water tap, tried opening it with her paw, and failed. Then she tried twisting it with her mouth—and accidentally broke it. Water splashed out, flooding the dining room.

Jimmy was in the playroom talking to Polly and Pines when he heard the sound of rushing water. He started walking toward it. Just then, Goldie ran out of the kitchen, panting and trying to hold the door shut.

"Goldie, could you move? I think I hear an open tap," Jimmy said.

Goldie blurted, "No! I mean… I farted in there and it's stinky! Don't go in!"

Jimmy knew something was wrong. He gently picked Goldie up in his mouth and set her aside. As he headed for the kitchen, the door burst open, sending a rush of water flooding into the playroom.

All the dogs panicked. Jimmy climbed onto a table.

"Dogs, we need to get out before Jenny returns! We can escape through the window into the lawn before it floods. You all know the way home—you came walking."

One dog asked, "But who did this?"

Jimmy paused. Goldie froze; afraid he would reveal her mistake. Instead, Jimmy said, "It was just a little accident when I tried to drink water. Don't get angry—let's focus on escaping."

Goldie was grateful. She looked at Jimmy with thankful eyes.

One by one, the dogs jumped out of the window into the lawn. Jimmy was the last to leave. He shut the window and told everyone to run home.

Just as he was about to leave, Jimmy heard a puppy screaming. A dog was trapped inside! He opened the window and jumped back in. The water reached his chin.

He saw Goldie standing on a table, worried.

"What happened? Why are you there?" Jimmy asked.

"I jumped here to make way for the others to escape, but now I'm trapped. The water is too high!"

Jimmy climbed onto the table and told Goldie to sit on his back. He jumped down, swimming through the water until they reached the window. He shut it tightly after escaping.

"Thank you!" Goldie said. "You rescued me and even took the blame for what I did."

Jimmy looked at her, then ran off. Goldie wanted to follow, but instead turned and walked slowly back to her house.

Later, Jenny returned to feed the dogs snacks. When she opened the door, water spilled out. She was shocked. Inside, the dogs were gone.

She called all the owners. Each said their dog had returned home drenched in water—except Ruhi, who said Jimmy hadn't come back.

Jenny rode her bicycle as fast as she could to Ruhi's house. Together, they searched the house with the help of the Chew Crew. Ruhi and Jenny searched the streets. Boba, Roxy, and July searched inside, while the triplets searched outside.

After thirty minutes, Nora found papers inside Jimmy's cage and a letter addressed "To the Chew Crew" in Jimmy's shaky handwriting. She called the others.

July suggested, "Maybe we should wait until Ruhi and Jenny come before reading it."

Roxy agreed. "It might say something we don't understand."

Boba argued, "But it's addressed to us. We can read it." Alice sided with Boba.

In the end, they decided to wait.

Ten minutes later, Ruhi returned. "Jenny went home and asked me to keep searching as she had to clean up the daycare," she said.

Nora showed her the papers. Ruhi unfolded one—it was a picture of some dogs. She recognized Jimmy, and the others looked familiar too.

The next was a sticky note: *"Escape the day you do something good."*

Another letter read:

To Jimmy

Dear Jimmy,

We have been trying to track your location by asking strays. We finally found you. Please return to us when you can. We miss you.

Love, Mom and Dad

Finally, they opened the last letter:

To the Chew Crew,

Dear Chew Crew, if you are reading this, it means I have left. I have tracked down my family—the dogs in the pictures. They live far away from the city, in the quiet outskirts. I decided I would return to them someday. I wanted to leave after doing something good, earning your trust, and leaving a happy memory.

I remember when I ran away and Ruhi found a poster of my parents searching for me. I remember her crying, and I overheard your conversations. I know I've been naughty and sometimes mean, so I think I should return to them. They miss me too.

I am living with my family now, but I will never forget you. You always cared for me, even when I wasn't kind. Thank you so much, Boba, Roxy, July, Alice, Nora, Rainbow, and Ruhi.

Love, Jimmy

Everyone understood. They were heartbroken. Alice, July, and Boba cried. Rainbow spoke aloud, as if Jimmy could hear:

"I'm so sorry, Jimmy. I'm glad you're living with your family."

Each of them repeated her words in turn.

After they cried for a while, Ruhi said, "Chew Crew, maybe we can visit him someday."

Everyone cheered. Though sad, they were happy for Jimmy.

8

Boba gets Ticks

It was a cloudy October afternoon. All the pets were getting their weekly bath and clean.

The triplets were washed in soup bowls and given neem twigs to chew on for their teeth.

July and Roxy were bathed in an inflatable pool with dog-friendly shampoo. Their collars and mini shoes were cleaned, and their teeth brushed and each of them had their fur blow-dried and sprayed with anti-tick spray. All except Boba!

He hadn't bathed or even been dry-cleaned for four months. He refused to be sprayed, combed, or shampooed. After one of his tantrums—where he even pulled Ruhi's hair—she gave up on trying to bathe him.

Later, the pets sat in the playroom in their fresh clothes and collars, playing cards.

"Hey, Crew! Let's play outside, I'm bored," Boba said.

July, who had just put down a card, replied, "We can play later. We just had a bath, and we'll get dirty if we go outside."

Rainbow added, “The weather isn’t nice either. It’s cloudy and looks like it might rain soon.”

“But I didn’t have a bath, and I’m bored!” Boba complained.

Alice suggested, “Why don’t you play outside in the park? We’ll join you after snacks or when it’s less cloudy.”

Boba frowned. “But I don’t want to play alone. That’s even more boring.”

Roxy, impatient for her turn, said, “Boba, why don’t you play with us?”

“But we always play cards! And it wouldn’t be fair if I joined now,” Boba argued.

Finally, quiet Nora spoke up. “Why don’t you spend some time with Ruhi? Her homework is done.”

Boba liked that idea and went upstairs.

Ruhi was lying on her bed, watching her phone. When she saw Boba, she smiled.

“Hi, Boba! Why aren’t you playing with the others?”

"They were only playing cards, and I wanted to play outside. So I thought I'd spend time with you," he said.

Ruhi laughed and petted him as he sat on her lap. When she playfully flipped open his ear, she spotted a strange round insect. She tried to pull it out, but it wouldn't budge.

"Boba, I think you have a tick," she said.

Boba shook his head. "It's probably just mud. I played in the mud yesterday."

Ruhi shrugged and went to the kitchen to give everyone some rusk.

The next day, after breakfast, everyone played in the park with their toys. They tried climbing a tree to catch a squirrel. Rainbow convinced Alice to help her build a circus rat cannon, but accidentally fired Alice into July—who was not amused.

They all got dirty, and before entering the house, Ruhi wiped them down with towels. Boba slipped inside unnoticed.

After lunch, Ruhi saw two more of the same insects near Boba's eye. When she asked, he insisted it was just dust. After some convincing, Ruhi believed him again.

That evening, Ruhi took all the pets for a walk. Boba, usually excited, was weak and tired. She noticed the insects had multiplied, almost covering his face and ears. She tugged one out with all her strength. When it finally came free, Boba whined, and the spot bled.

Ruhi now knew for sure—it was a tick.

She called the vet, but he was on vacation. The nurse advised her to separate Boba until the vet returned. Ruhi cleaned Jimmy's cage and placed Boba inside.

For two days, Boba grew weaker. More ticks appeared. When one fell out, he bled and howled in pain.

Finally, the vet returned. Ruhi carried Boba to the clinic. The vet plucked out the larger ticks with tweezers and wrapped him in bandages.

"It's good you separated him," the vet said. "Otherwise, the other pets—and even you—could have gotten them. Make sure he bathes weekly and gets sprayed with anti-tick medicine. Even if he hates it, you must do it. He should eat healthy food and rest. I'm giving him a cone so he doesn't lick his scars."

Back home, the Crew didn't tease Boba. They knew he was hurt. For days, he stayed quiet, barely eating or playing.

After a week, the bandages and cone were removed. The first thing Boba did was jump into the inflatable pool and happily get sprayed with anti-tick spray.

From that day on, Boba always looked forward to baths. It wasn't just about staying tick-free anymore—he had learned that sometimes, a little discomfort leads to a lot of good.

9

A Day at the Mall

It was a cold morning. The Chew Crew were helping Rainbow make a pet phone out of broken plastic bits, a battery, and some cardboard. Rainbow and July worked on the design, Alice and Roxy decorated, while Boba and Nora built.

They thought it would be a normal day until Ruhi entered the room. "Crew, come on! I need to get you all ready—we're going to the mall today!" she announced, calling all the pets to the playroom.

Ruhi dressed them up - Boba wore a blue hat with holes for his ears, July wore a pink scarf, Roxy had butterfly-shaped clips on her ears and the triplets wore matching brown sweaters.

Ruhi placed the triplets in her purse and decided not to take leashes for the dogs—it would be too hard to hold three at once. They booked a taxi and climbed inside.

When they arrived, they had a small snack before hopping off to shop. Ruhi first visited a pet store, buying new collars for the dogs, clothes for the rats, and tiny shoes to keep their feet warm in winter. She visited a few more shops, picking up treats, toys, and bowls customized with their names.

The Crew were thrilled and couldn't wait to play with their new things. After about an hour of shopping, they had lunch at the pet-friendly food court on the terrace.

Ruhi checked the time—it was 3:00 p.m. She needed to be home by 6:00 to finish her homework. "Pets, we can go to one more shop, then we'll take a taxi home, okay?" she said.

The Crew agreed. They went up to a higher floor and spotted a big, brightly lit new store. Neon lights and music instantly caught their attention.

Ruhi walked in, wide-eyed at the shelves filled with teddy bears, hobby kits, stationery, and more. She saw a beautiful white backpack and wanted to buy it, but when she checked her pocket, she realized she only had enough money left for the taxi home.

"Maybe next time…" she muttered.

As she walked out, she bumped into a school friend. They began chatting, and Ruhi signaled to the pets to wait nearby.

Alice whispered, "Crew, come here for a second. Ruhi bought us so many things, but nothing for herself."

Roxy said, "Maybe we should buy her that white bag she wanted!"

July replied sarcastically, "And where do we get the money for that?"

Boba suggested, "Let's walk around the shop. Maybe we'll get an idea!"

Soon, they reached the noisy kids' section. Many tired children were crying and screaming while their parents looked annoyed.

Nora said, "I have an idea! What if we put on a show to distract the kids? Maybe their parents will give us money." Rainbow hesitated. "That's a weird idea… but it might work."

Meanwhile, Ruhi finished talking to her friend and realized the pets weren't where she had asked them to stay. Worried, she asked the cashier, "Have you seen some dogs or rats go anywhere?" The cashier shook his head. Ruhi decided to look around the store.

The Chew Crew were already performing. Boba wagged his tail so hard it looked like dancing. July spun in circles nonstop. Roxy chased her tail and tripped. The triplets performed gymnastics.

Soon, the children stopped crying and gathered to watch. Their parents followed. When the show ended, July and Roxy sat facing each other, while Boba stood on two legs, resting his paws on their heads. The triplets hung from his wagging tail. The crowd clapped loudly.

Alice jumped off Boba's tail, pulled off his cap, and held it upside down. People dropped money inside. When the crowd dispersed, the Crew counted—it was just enough for the bag.

Boba carried the cap in his mouth while Roxy grabbed the bag from the shelf. They ran to the billing counter, now empty. Alice jumped up and placed the cap with the money on the counter. July handed the bag to the cashier.

Just then, Ruhi arrived, searching for them. When she saw the Crew handing over money and the bag she had wanted, she ran and hugged them.

While the cashier billed the bag and the pets' items, the Crew explained how they had earned the money. The cashier, listening with a smile, said, "That is so sweet! Don't tell anyone, but I'll give you 60% off because of how loyal and thoughtful you are."

Ruhi beamed. "Thank you so much!"

The cashier handed them their bags. With money left over, the Crew had another idea. Before catching a taxi, they bought popsicles—all watermelon flavor.

Tired but happy, they sang all the way home. Ruhi thanked the driver for tolerating the noisy bunch.

10

The Best Pet

It was a sunny day, and all the pets were quietly playing in the playroom. July and Boba were chasing each other in a game of tag, Alice was playing with dolls, Nora was reading a book about leaves, Roxy was chewing on a slipper she had found, and Rainbow was writing in a notebook. She didn't show anyone what she was writing, insisting it was a secret. When she finished, she grinned, closed the book, jumped onto a cardboard box, and announced, "Crew, according to my calculations, I am the best pet in the Chew Crew."

July stopped chasing Boba and growled. "Best? No, I'm the best!"

Roxy yipped, "Everyone loves puppies. That's why I'm the best pet."

Nora looked up from her book and said calmly, "You need a pet like me—quiet and smart. That makes me the best."

Boba licked himself proudly, as if giving himself a kiss. "I'm the most energetic dog ever! I'm the best pet."

Alice put down her dolls and declared, "I'm silly—err, I mean cute and talented! The perfect friend!"

Rainbow had an idea. "Let's settle this with a competition. Six rounds, each of us creates one. Ruhi can be the judge. But there's one rule—you can't compete in the round you design." Everyone agreed excitedly.

The Crew brainstormed ideas and, a few minutes later, went down to the lawn with ribbons, cloth, and a clipboard with paper and pen. They decorated a small section of the lawn and called Ruhi, who agreed to judge. She wrote down the competitions they had created:

Competition one: Rusk Machine – July

Whoever eats three rusks the fastest wins. Rats only need to eat one.

Competition two: Ribbon Race – Boba

Whoever runs the fastest with two legs tied together wins. Rats run only a quarter of the distance.

Competition three: Leaf Hunt – Roxy

Whoever finds a heart-shaped leaf first wins.

Competition four: Nine-Piece Puzzle – Rainbow Whoever finds the missing piece to the puzzle first wins.

Competition five: Nose Balance – Nora

Whoever balances a ball on their nose the longest wins. Rats use marbles instead of tennis balls.

Competition six: Block Stack – Alice

Whoever stacks the most building blocks without the tower falling wins. Rats can climb pulleys if the tower gets too tall.

With everything ready, the competitions began.

For the Rusk Machine, July sat beside Ruhi while she laid out bundles of rusks. Ruhi gave July one so she wouldn't feel left out. Into her pink microphone connected to a speaker,

Ruhi announced, "Welcome to the Best Pet Competitions 2026! Our first round is the Rusk Machine by July. Ready? Three... two... one... go!"

Boba's big mouth gave him an advantage. While everyone else finished one rusk (the rats managing just over a quarter), Boba had already eaten two. He quickly finished all three and won the round.

Ruhi wrote his name on the clipboard and announced the next round, the Ribbon Race.

"On your mark, get set, go!" Roxy sprinted with incredible speed, managing to keep the ribbon tying her front legs intact. Nora would have won, but was stunned by Roxy's speed and stopped mid-race. Roxy crossed the finish line, panting heavily, and Ruhi shouted, "Roxy wins the Ribbon Race!"

Next was the Leaf Hunt. "Three… two… one… go!" Ruhi called. Everyone scattered, except Nora, who remembered from her book that peepal trees had heart-shaped leaves. She ran to the old peepal tree, picked up a leaf from the ground, and brought it to Ruhi. "Nora wins this round!" Ruhi announced.

Rainbow's Nine-Piece Puzzle came next. "You must assemble the puzzle, then find the missing piece. Ready? Go!"

July and Alice worked quickly, but July sniffed the puzzle and followed its scent. She found the missing piece before anyone else and proudly handed it to Ruhi. "July wins!"

Then came Nose Balance. Ruhi handed out balls and marbles. "Ready? Three… two… one… go!" Alice stayed perfectly still, determined to win. Roxy sneezed and dropped her ball, Boba got distracted by a squirrel, July jumped when a fly landed on her head, Rainbow dropped hers while attempting a backflip, and Nora fell asleep, snoring the marble off her nose. Alice remained steady and won the round.

Finally, it was time for Block Stack. Ruhi placed blocks next to a tray. "Three… two… one… go!" Nora and Roxy used pulleys and boxes to stack their towers, while Rainbow jumped high enough to place blocks easily. Boba and July accidentally knocked theirs down, Nora got stuck after jumping off her box, and Roxy threw a stone at her tower just to see what would happen. Rainbow's tower stood tallest with twelve blocks. "Rainbow wins!" Ruhi announced.

All the pets gathered under a big tree for the final results. Ruhi smiled. “The winner and the best pet are…” The Crew held their breath. “All of you!”

The pets gasped. “Huh?”

Ruhi explained, “I can’t choose just one best or favorite pet. You’re all amazing in different ways, and I love you equally. I declare all of you the best pets! You’re not just the best pets—you’re my best friends.”

The Crew cheered happily and went inside, feeling proud. That evening, they had a party to celebrate. Ruhi giggled to herself, “I’m the best daughter—the only daughter!”

PHOTO GALLERY

Bengaluru 27 December 2025 at 16:14

Roxy

Verses Kindler Publication

Verses Kindler Publication

Reach us through our website -

https://www.verseskindlerpublication.com/

For more information visit our

Instagram or Facebook page